MY GOLDEN QUILL

M. FARHAAN HUSSAIN

To my Mother -

Thank you for inspiring me to passionately weave stories and
bring out this book.

Contents

PREFACE

"Short stories are tiny windows into other worlds and other minds and other dreams." - Neil Gaiman

I open these tiny windows to my young readers through 'My Golden Quill'. The greatest pleasure for me is writing short stories and poems which convey a message, kindle your thoughts and imagination. I hope you will enjoy reading each piece just as I enjoyed writing them.

I

MY GOLDEN QUILL

In the northern part of the city was a large forest land owned by an ornithologist, Dr. Rammoorthy. He had bought the forest land a decade ago. His forest would attract different varieties of birds and he would study them closely.

Once during his morning walk in the forest, he found a sparkling Golden Parakeet. His excitement knew no bounds as this species was believed to have gone extinct hundreds of years ago. As he tried to get closer, it flew away leaving behind its quill. Ram was keenly observing the beautiful quill when a strong gust of wind blew outside carrying the quill with it.

The quill flew for long and finally dropped in the hands of an artistic baker, Linda. Linda had recently received an order for a forest themed cake and used this quill to give the cake a beautiful finishing touch. Once it was ready, she delivered the cake to Mr. Rajan who had ordered it for his son's birthday.

The birthday party was filled with fun and joy. Rajan's son had invited all his friends and they were having a wonderful time. When it was time to cut the cake, Rajan's son blew the candles and the quill got blown away. It flew far and settled on a lush green lawn.

Della Regent was completely engrossed in the sequins catalogue in her lawn, when her eyes fell on the beautiful quill and she couldn't stop admiring its beauty. Della was a famous fashion designer and currently she was designing a wedding gown for the wealthy businessman, Jeeva Rangarajan's daughter. Della tugged in the quill to make the wedding gown more elegant.

It was the wedding day! There was a huge gathering of guests and the venue was royally decorated. It was a very grand celebration. All eyes were set on the beautiful gown of the bride and everyone showered their praises. When the bride passed by an air cooler, the dash of air carried the quill away from the gown.

The quill now landed in the hands of a small boy who was playing in the park. He found the quill very pretty and kept it in his pocket. While he was playing, the quill fell down on the soft green grass of the park. A mother crow who was in search of twigs came across it. She was attracted by its beauty. The quill was perfect for her baby crows to cuddle in. One morning, when her babies were learning to fly by spluttering their wings, the quill fell from the nest landing inside a beautiful gift bag.

My uncle brought along the gift bag as he reached home. He did not notice that a quill had fallen into the bag. He wanted to surprise me with a gift as he was visiting me after many years. When I opened the gift, I was very excited to find my favourite books and a sparkling golden quill in the bag. On seeing the quill, my grandpa told me that in the olden days people used quills to write. They would dip the tip of the quill in ink and write with it.

This quill has since become my best companion. It keeps giving new ideas for my stories. So, this is the story of "My Golden Quill". Its journey now continues with the many stories that I narrate through this book.

II

A SAFARI THROUGH KABINI

A bright Sunday morning and I was eagerly waiting for the safari at the Kabini National Park. It was a pleasant day after the night's drizzle and the climate was perfect as we boarded the jeep with the other visitors. The leaves of the trees were covered with dewdrops. The path was filled with slush and the jeep jumped through the puddles all the way to the safari camp.

The safari vehicles were ready and all of us boarded it. The guide welcomed us, introduced himself, provided the visitors with a pair of binoculars and briefed us with the rules and tips. We were glad to know that the others accompanying us on the safari included a wildlife photographer, a travelogue writer, wildlife enthusiasts and a couple of them from the National Geographic team. All the safari vehicles started *together but a little later each took a different path inside the forest. Our vehicle was moving through the thick forest and we were looking eagerly in every direction to sight the wild animals, birds in their natural habitat. All the guides of the safari vehicles communicated whenever they sighted the large animals.*

In the serenity of the forest, we could hear the peacock, the cuckoo and the insects. Suddenly, a brown animal crossed our path. It was a mongoose, the first animal we sighted in the safari. We continued moving ahead and spotted peacocks, other birds and many small animals. It was a pleasure to sight animals in the forest. We clicked photographs of the animals. The forest was filled with the melodious chirping of the birds but all this was disturbed with a loud cry.

We looked through our binoculars and spotted a watering hole on the other side of the bushes. A baby elephant was stuck in the muddy watering hole and was crying for help. The elephant herd was not seen nearby. Our guide immediately informed the forest authorities and the team arrived swiftly. We also joined to lend a helping hand and got to witness the rescue of the calf. The baby elephant squealed with joy. We all patted this cute baby elephant and it went in search of its herd. We returned back to our vehicle and the safari continued.

The sky was getting darker as the sun made way for the clouds and then there was a sudden downpour. The driver turned the vehicle towards the next spot. The path was filled with puddles and the ride was more like a roller-coaster causing all of us to grab the seats, sometimes falling over the left or to the right and at times even jumping off the seat. We were enjoying the rain and the joy ride, when our guide got a quick tip off that a leopard has been sighted. The vehicle turned in that direction and sped to reach the spot. We were curious as we got closer to the spot.

When we reached the spot, our guide informed us that the mother leopard has just gone chasing its prey, but the baby leopard has climbed the tree and is resting on its branch taking shelter from rain. We reached out for our binoculars and cameras. Spotting the leopard in its natural habitat, it was a sight to behold. Cameras clicked this precious moment. We waited to check if the mother leopard would be back anytime soon. Our guide got to know it was not sighted anywhere in the vicinity, so the safari started off for the camp.

The rain stopped and near a lake, we spotted a pack of wild dogs feasting on their prey. Our guide also helped us sight a herd of elephants amidst the huge forest trees. We could hear the sounds of the elephants and felt as if they were thanking us for rescuing their calf.

Our vehicle was now racing ahead to reach the camp before it gets dark. We returned to our resort having completed a memorable, fun-filled and adventurous forest safari.

III
CYCLE

It races on the road,
It speeds up with the wind,
It chases the clouds,
It zooms past the crowd!
It is my best friend,
Our friendship will never end,
I travel on it daily,
It ensures that I reach safely!
It rides so swiftly,
It helps me reach quickly!
It keeps me fit and healthy,
It makes my day jolly and merry!

IV
A SCOUT'S ADVENTURE

Robert Williams was a brave hunter and had ventured into the Jabalpur Forest on the orders of the Maharajah, to capture a man-eating leopard. When he did not return for a week, the Forest guards started searching for him but the forest was so deep and dense that the search was abandoned after a few days.

Many years later...

Rahul, an adventurous and bright boy danced with joy when his father gave his consent for him to join the adventure-filled scouts. The scouts were to camp in the Jabalpur Forest. Rahul's father, Mr. Vivek allowed his son to join the scouts just in the nick of time as the registrations closed the next day.

The scouts were departing three days after the registrations closed and Rahul spent his time daydreaming about the fun he would have with his scout mates at the campsite. He was very excited! Three days passed in a flash and Rahul was ready with his things packed in a backpack.

The minivan arrived with many young scouts, who were very excited to spend a few days of their summer vacation, camping in a forest. Rahul boarded the minivan and it passed through the bustling city and reached the entrance of the marvellous Jabalpur Forest. The scouts marched in with their leader, General Smith, and stopped at a spot with sufficient sunlight. The General selected that spot for camping. The tents were placed and wood was arranged to light up the campfire in the evening. This was just the beginning as the General had loads of adventurous tasks lined up for his team!

Rahul thoroughly enjoyed completing the tasks and winning badges from the General. He always waited for the evenings as the General narrated humorous stories during the campfires. He also eagerly waited for his turn for the food-gathering task. The General sent one scout each day to gather food for the whole group.

Rahul finally got his turn. Unfortunately, it had rained heavily the day before and wild trees covered *the paths. The growth of wild trees made it difficult for him to navigate and consequently, he lost his way. At the campsite, the General was worried as Rahul did not return by late evening.*

Rahul got scared when he heard howls, then growls, and finally, roars echoing in his ears. He ran as fast as he could to get away from the spot but as he ran, he went deeper and deeper into the forest. After a while, he stopped and started panting. Just as he turned his head, to his surprise, he saw a house lit up with lanterns and surrounded with blossoms. To escape the cold, he climbed up the dusty stairs and gathered the courage to knock on the door. A man opened it and its creaking sound scared Rahul. The man with a kind smile welcomed him. He felt comfortable with the stranger. Then, a thunder blew away the silence and the raindrops gushed in.

The stranger led Rahul through the hallway which was adorned with portraits of the long-lost Hunter Williams. The man introduced himself as Johnson and pushed open a door. On entering the room, Rahul could feel the warmth of the fireplace. He was made to sit on a cosy couch by the fireplace and fell asleep in a short while.

Meanwhile, the General went to the Forest Officer and reported regarding the disappearance of Rahul. The night passed away with heavy rains. The next morning, Johnson woke Rahul up. When he opened his eyes, he saw a growling leopard beside Johnson. Rahul got frightened out of his wits and just then another man entered the room. He calmed him down and said that the leopard doesn't harm the people visiting his mansion.

Rahul found a few leopard cubs playing in the corner and tried touching one. Rahul looked up at the man who had just entered and his jaw dropped to see the great hunter, Robert Williams.

Williams said, "She's Greta. The leopard I had once set out to kill." Rahul then asked, "...and you never returned?". "No, because when I encountered her, I understood the reason why she harmed the people.", said the great hunter. "I saw her that day, she was right in front of my eyes. I held my bullet, aimed at her, and shot her without even waiting for a moment to understand her. She was strong enough and remained alive but dropped to the ground due to the injury. That's when her three cubs came rushing from the bushes. I then understood what had made her a 'man-eater'.

She killed the poachers who did not respect the animals' privacy and, of course, she had the protection of her babies in her mind. I ran to her and took my first aid kit to relieve her of the pain." Rahul was teary eyed as he got really inspired by Robert Williams. Hunter Robert then lived with his trusted aide Johnson in an abandoned mansion deep inside the Jabalpur Forest. This hunter who was once hated by animals was now the friend of all species present in the forest. He now *dedicated himself to the protection of the animals.*

He offered Rahul a healthy breakfast of plums, coconut water, and fish. Then, he led Rahul to the campsite through the bushes so no one discovers him. Before bidding farewell, the hunter said to Rahul, "Listen, young fella! You are the inspiration for this world. Spread the message that we cannot survive without nature. The creatures we call animals are not harmful instead we're the ones who spread pollution, ruin forests through deforestation and put our lives at risk by destroying nature. Now, off you go!"

Rahul was happy to have learned a great lesson to share with his friends and left to join the scouts. When he returned, his scout mates and the General were glad and relieved to see Rahul back. It was the last day of camping and the minivan had come again to take them back to their homes.

Rahul got back home, freshened himself up, and narrated his adventure to his family. His father who was with the Wildlife Protection Committee couldn't believe that Williams who was believed to have been killed by a man-eater was alive. He thought Rahul must have seen a strange dream. But, when he heard Rahul's story, he was happy that the person in Rahul's 'dream' taught him something important that the world must understand. Well, let's hope we all learn to conserve nature and spread Hunter Williams' message to the society.

V
POLLUTION

How harmful is pollution,
it destroys the peaceful, healthy life
of each and every living creation,
As we are the ones continuously spreading this situation,
we need to think of a better solution!
How quickly we are polluting the air,
making clean air rare!
Letting out the waste into the water,
we are making survival harder,
Filling up the earth with garbage,
we destroy every inch of our motherland!
I plead everyone to lend a helping hand,
To stop the pollution all over the land,
which can again be made beautiful and grand.
Pollution disturbs nature,
troubling each and every creature.
May we succeed in reducing pollution!
May we soon stop this spreading situation!

VI
THE PARAGLIDING ADVENTURE

Marco and Ronny lived in Rio. Their father was famous for his excellent performance in sport. He had always wanted his children to also do something great like him. They too loved sport.

One day, they tried paragliding and enjoyed it. On seeing them enjoy it a lot, their parents decided to encourage them to go ahead with the sport. They attended training, their coaches liked their confidence and amazing performance and soon, they were declared proficient students.

On their birthday, they were gifted a pair of gliders with the safety set. They took part in many competitions, won many awards and the Government recognized their talent. Their father was proud of them. Once, while taking part in a competition, they were having a wonderful time gliding in the sky but then a strong wind blew their paragliders towards the west direction, instead of the north! Marco and Ronny tried their best to control it but their efforts went in vain. Soon, the weather got very chilly for them and they fainted in exhaustion. They were gliding away from the hills and finally their gliders landed in a tribal village.

The village was amidst a thick forest with tall trees and treehouses of wood and bamboo upon every tree. The noise of the gliders crashing frightened the villagers. They looked out through their windows but remained safe inside their treehouses. The chief then decided to visit the strangers. Seeing Marco and Ronny badly hurt, the chief attended to their wounds. When they woke up, they screamed in fright seeing many people staring at them closely. The chief calmed them down and was very friendly. Marco and Ronny breathed a sigh of relief.

The chief saw their glider, equipment and their first aid kit. He thought that they could help his tribes as they possessed smart equipment. He told them about the biggest problem the villagers were facing, the dragon. According to the history of the village, the ancestors of the chief found a safe environment in this forest. They were unaware of the fact that a dangerous dragon had his home in the same forest. The dragon was angry and wanted the tribes to leave his abode but then he smelt the aroma of food being cooked in their kitchen. The dragon was really hungry and deprived of food for several weeks. He allowed the tribes to live in the forest with the condition that they offer him food.

The dragon enjoyed the delicious food prepared by the tribes. He enjoyed every meal but soon greed took over his mind. The tribes paid lots of respect to the dragon and the dragon took advantage of the tribes' kindness. He threatened that if the tribes did not provide food to his entire group, he would set fire to the forest.

The tribes did not have enough people and resources. They would work hard tilling the land, hunting, fishing etc. They had to use up a lot of their limited resources and fresh produce to satisfy the need of the dragons. Marco and Ronny tried to think of a solution to their problem. They gathered some tribe warriors to help them in teaching the dragons a lesson so they would never again trouble the tribes. They taught the warriors how to make catapults and spears. They also trained them in using the weapons. When the dragons arrived for their feast, they struck them with their catapults. The dragons lost their balance and then they hit their spears on them. The dragons became very weak after the sudden attack and were overpowered.

Marco and Ronny explained to the dragons that the size of the tribes was smaller than the dragons and gathering the resources required days and nights of hard work. The dragons realized that the villagers worked really hard to gather the resources the dragons spent on their greed.

The dragons' greed blew away and their heart felt an affectionate change. They promised to never trouble the tribes again and instead, help them in their daily chores. The chief, the dragons and the whole town thanked Marco and Ronny. The chief arranged a traditional dance performance and a grand feast for all. Marco and Ronny then requested the chief to help them return home. The dragons agreed to fly them back home. The whole village waved them good-bye.

They returned to Rio and narrated their adventure to everyone back home. It was an adventure they could never forget! It was an adventure that helped them learn that there is sufficiency in the world for everyone's need but not for everyone's greed!

VII
MIRROR

It reflects our happiness,
It tells us to smile and spread joy!
It reflects our sorrow,
It tells us to wipe out our cries.
It reflects our mistakes,
It shows us where we went wrong,
It tells us to rectify our mistakes.
It reflects our life,
It shows us our aim,
It tells us to continue walking on the path filled with goodness,
And work hard till we achieve our goals.
It reflects our journey,
It shows us from where we started in our lives and
where we are today,
It tells us to continue to progress and prosper!

VIII
BELLA'S JOURNEY

George was staring at the walls of his home; they were adorned with photo frames. Each of these frames had memories of George with his pet dog, Bella. These two best friends could never be parted. One day, George had lost Bella in the park during his morning walk. George had tied Bella to the lamp post while he was busy attending a call. A beautiful butterfly had come fluttering by and Bella couldn't resist the temptation to catch it. Her collar gave away and she was now chasing the butterfly.

George wasn't paying attention as he was on the call for his first job interview. Bella stopped when the butterfly settled on a flowerpot placed in a truck. Bella entered through the wide entrance and was just about to pounce on the butterfly when it got totally dark. The butterfly escaped through a tiny hole when the truck's doors were being locked. Bella was trapped! She had no idea where she was traveling in that truck.

Meanwhile, in the park, George was worried! His dear Bella was missing. He returned home after searching for Bella the whole day. But he didn't lose hope. Soon, he got to know that a few people had spotted Bella near the florist's place. The florist said, "I remember seeing a dog. She was chasing a butterfly near my truck loaded with Sunflowers. It was an order to be delivered to Mrs. Malini in Ashok Nagar." The florist thought for a while and added that it's possible that Bella would have boarded the truck. They immediately contacted the truck driver to find out if he had seen Bella. The driver said, "When I opened the truck door, a dog pounced on me. I panicked and it ran away. It might be Bella!"

George was saddened at the thought of having lost Bella and with no clue on how to locate her. He called his friends and sought their help in finding Bella. Few of his friends were kind enough to volunteer and search for Bella.

Meanwhile, Bella was confused. She had no idea how to get back home! Since it was getting dark, she made herself comfortable under the shade of a huge banyan tree. The next day, a traffic policeman who was posted nearby found Bella. He saw that Bella was hungry. He kindly patted her, offered her food, and called the Animal Rescue Centre who helped the lost dogs.

George and his friends started enquiring with others from all parts of the city. They did not get any lead for *a week. George was getting anxious with every passing day. After many tireless attempts, one of George's friends, Anita, got to know from a traffic policeman that he had found a pet dog and had called the Animal Rescue Team to help the dog.*

Anita rushed to the Rescue Centre and got to know from the officer that they had waited for a week for the owner to claim the rescued dog. When they did not hear from the owner, they had given the dog for adoption. He further added that their privacy policy does not allow them to share the contact details of the person who had adopted the dog. Anita pleaded with him but in vain.

Anita informed George regarding her visit to the Rescue Centre. On hearing about her conversation with the officer, George decided to visit the Animal Rescue Centre himself the next morning. He went straight to the officer's cabin and spoke to him regarding Bella. The officer felt helpless when George showed him some photographs as proof that he was the rightful owner of Bella. Dejected, George left the place. Meanwhile, Bella found her new owner, Ajay to be as loving, kind, and caring as George. As no one visited his house, Bella could figure out that Ajay was living alone and loved to have some company at his home. Ajay had found something special in Bella when he saw her at the Rescue Centre. He felt as if he had finally found a loving companion to spend time with and immediately adopted her.

It was ten days since George had lost Bella and she was still not found. Depressed, George decided to visit the park again. The park brought back the memories of his morning walks with Bella playing around the bushes and the children there. As he recollected his memories, he saw a man walking with Bella. George rubbed his eyes thinking that it was a dream! He was hesitant to approach the man because he knew that there was the possibility that it could also be a dog that resembled Bella. George was confused! Just then Bella spotted George and came running to him. Ajay then approached George and apologized for his dog's behaviour.

Ajay turned to head back to his home, but Bella refused to accompany Ajay and sat on George's boots. George then explained the entire story of how his pet Bella had gone missing and landed up at the Animal Rescue Centre. Ajay could understand that George loved Bella a lot and he wanted her back but Ajay found it difficult to part with his new friend. Ajay knew that his life would be lonely once again, but knowing that George had brought up Bella as a small puppy, he finally decided to give Bella back to George.

Being reunited with Bella, George's happiness knew no bounds! He called up all his friends and threw a party at his home. Meanwhile Ajay again started searching for a companion which he could bring home and spend time with. Luckily, one bright morning, while watering the plants in his garden, he heard a bird chirping. He looked around and found a beautiful green parrot singing from a branch of the mango tree in his garden. The mango tree bore no fruit and realizing that the parrot was in search of food, Ajay offered it a few ripe mangoes. The parrot relished the mangoes and was so happy that it started flying around Ajay in delight. Ajay finally found a new friend in his life, Polly, his pet parrot!

IX
MESSENGERS IN THE SKY

Birds and clouds,
These are the messengers in the sky,
They spread goodwill and cheer,
As they move from one continent to another!
They spread happiness and delight,
As they travel day and night!
With their peace and charm,
They make our day bright and warm!
They light up the sky,
They spread merry and joy!!

X

THE HAUNTED HOUSE

All of us sat in a circle and were in deep thoughts. We were looking for a perfect open space where we could have our game of cricket. The playground was pre-occupied by the seniors who were having their football matches. We couldn't play in our compound as we already had a record of smashing our neighbour, Mr Kumar's windows with our hits! Just then, Aditya remembered Mr Douglas' house as it had a large garden.

Mr Douglas was a retired army officer who had shifted to Florida in the United States with his only daughter, Amanda. It had been a decade since he left India and his house was left unattended, filled with cobwebs, dust and slush. The patches of algae gave the walls, which were once bright white, an ugly dull green coating. Rumour had spread around town that his house was haunted. A week ago, a traveller passing by his house had heard mysterious sounds. The night was cold and the frightening sounds gave him the shivers that he ran as fast as he could. The district collector's secretary lived nearby. One evening, while returning home from the collectorate, he saw a bright light from one of the windows of Mr Douglas' house. He stopped his bike and looked more closely only to find a white body with a frightening face and flaring red eyes. He got so scared that he lost balance and fell off his bike. A few passers-by helped him get back home. He fell ill with fever for a week.

A news reporter who bravely went in to report on this 'Haunted House' never returned back. This had frightened the people as well as the policemen who started believing in ghosts. These incidents terrified the common commuters who avoided that road for travel. But the boys of the local cricket club were brave and they were not worried as they were planning to play only in the garden and not enter the house. It was a tough match between the local cricket club, Chennai Champions led by Aditya and Madras Marvels led by Raghu.

The Champions won the toss and elected to field. In the initial overs, Marvels' opening batsmen scored huge runs but Siddharth got the crucial wickets for our Chennai Champions. The match was really interesting and finally, it was the last ball! The Marvels made 120 runs in 19.5 overs with 5 wickets. Prasanth was a fast bowler and he bowled his best ball at the captain of the Marvels, Raghu Swaminathan. Raghu's eyes were at the ball. He swung his bat and the ball flew in the air and smash! A large glass window of the house was shattered to pieces and the ball landed inside. The ball was a new one and it was a shiny red cricket ball. The ball belonged to Prasanth. Aditya's team protested that Raghu should go in and get it. But Raghu's team disagreed. They claimed that Prasanth threw a strong ball and it was not Raghu's fault.

A loud sound interrupted the discussion among the teams. It was a scary and frightening voice. The noise of the shattering of the glass window had triggered the ghosts! They busted out of the door and came out in the garden to scare away the trespassers. They were bright white in colour and their light illuminated the grass around them. Their eyes were blood red and deadly! They were floating in the air and laughing loudly on seeing our players shiver with fear.

Prasanth was a witty boy. He saw that the ghosts had left the door open and were distracted in scaring his teammates. So, he hatched up a simple plan to bring back his cricket ball. Slowly but carefully, he crept towards Aditya and dragged him along. The ghosts didn't notice their movement. Prasanth then told Aditya about his intention to get back the ball and Aditya joined him.

They entered the house and a strong wind hit the doors and windows. The creaking sound of the doors distracted the ghosts. The moment the ghosts turned around towards the doors, Raghu and the other players made their way out through the gate. They ran as fast as they could, looking back every minute to ensure that the ghosts weren't chasing them. The ghosts just wanted them out and had no intention of following them.

Aditya and Prasanth hid behind the door as the ghosts returned back to the house. Just then, Aditya noticed something in the ghosts. They had a black band with propellers at four corners on their heads. He then remembered his big brother, a student of Engineering, using such a component in his projects. He remembered; it was a 'drone' that could fly in the air with its propellers. He then wondered if the ghosts were real or if they were invented to scare others. He went inside along with Prasanth. They saw a few computers connected together and discovered that these were used to track the drones.

Aditya had learnt all about electronics from his brother, Nishant. He also noticed a lever. He pulled it towards the west, the ghosts came to his left. If he brought it towards the east, the ghosts came towards his right. There was another lever. He turned it towards the north, the ghosts moved upwards and when in the opposite direction, they moved downwards. He then understood that the ghosts were triggered by sound as well as the movement of the lever remote. Someone wanted the people to stay away from Mr Douglas' house. But who could it be? It was the big question in Aditya and Prasanth's minds. As they were walking ahead, to explore more secrets about the haunted house, they were lost in their thoughts – Who would want people to stay away from this old house?

Suddenly the floor beneath them broke open into a secret path downwards. They were caught unawares and they fell into the path moving downwards. They tried to remain silent but couldn't help and screamed due to the sudden fall. Three men who were having a conversation in the basement got alerted by the scream. They got up, pushed open the curtain which hid their room and stepped out towards the secret path to catch the trespassers. The scare had left Prasanth unconscious but Aditya dragged him to a corner and hid behind a box. The men looked around but noticed no one. They thought that the path must have opened up due to the wind and they would have heard the noise from outside. Just for safety, they went up through the path to have a look in the garden.

Meanwhile, Aditya started observing the secret room and noticed two men tied to a pillar with a rope and their mouths covered with a cloth. Aditya recognized them, they were the missing news reporter and his cameraperson, Rob Francis and Anant Varma of the National News Network. They were in deep sleep. Aditya woke them up and they realized that he was there to rescue them. Aditya loosened their rope and hid them behind the box with Prasanth. Francis and Varma understood his intention to remain hidden. The three men returned back. They were so busy in their conversation that they did not notice that Francis and Varma had escaped. Francis thanked Aditya for rescuing him and said that he fell into the secret path while reporting about this house that was believed to be haunted. Being an expert detective and news reporter, he explored the basement he had landed into and had recorded the entire conversation of the men hiding there. He had also gathered information that they were poachers in secret talks with illegal traders who traded in the specimens of endangered flora and fauna. These men bribed the forest officers and illegally hunted endangered species of animals including lions, tigers and even elephants!

The corrupt forest officers assigned to protect nature violated their duties and instead helped the poachers go unnoticed. These men then used the hides and fur of the animals to make expensive clothes and sold their horns and tusks as collectables. They had caught Francis when his phone rang but Varma managed to run from the scene. As he was running, he slipped over some sand and he was caught too. Their phones were switched off and the camera was seized.

Francis then asked Prasanth to secretly search the first floor of the house to get more clues. Prasanth secretly searched the wardrobes on the first floor and found clothes made from the fur of the poached animals. Prasanth also found their cricket ball and a camera. He opened a desk where he also managed to find the mobile phones of Francis and Varma. He then came downstairs where he met Aditya, Francis and Varma who had managed to reach the ground floor.

They all exited the house and went to the police station. They narrated the incident and showed the video to the Commissioner. A police team was sent to the house to carry out the investigation. They surrounded the house and captured the poachers. They also seized all the illegal goods. Meanwhile, the corrupt forest officers who helped the poachers were caught and severely punished.

Prasanth and Aditya were honoured by the police as well as by their school for their bravery. Francis and Varma also received accolades for their excellent reporting. The next day, the Chennai Champions and the Madras Marvels faced each other once again for their next match. Before they started a new match, they all applauded for Prasanth and Aditya. They all agreed that though their previous match was abandoned halfway, Prasanth and Aditya were the true winners of the match.

XI
CHALLENGES

Challenges give you a test,
They bring out your best!
Challenges strengthen you;
They extend your limits!
Challenges are daring;
They make life interesting!
Challenges give you the best rewards;
They help you break records!
Challenges help you realize your potential;
They make you reach the pinnacle!
Challenges build your character;
They help you break every barrier!
They make you smarter and wiser!

XII

ADVENTURES AT ANDAMAN

It was a much-awaited vacation. The sound of the waves echoed around us. The cool breeze was a relief from the heat. I and my family were at the Andaman Coast. We had come to visit our dear Grandpa who was turning 70 this year. Me and my cousin, Zoya, had booked a scuba diving session for ourselves. We were really excited to explore the wonders of the Andaman Sea!

We wore our suits, put on our goggles, and sailed in the boats. When we reached the spot, we attached the oxygen cylinders to our backs and dived into the sea. The coral reefs welcomed us with a colourful aura. There were a variety of fishes, big and small, fast and slow, swimming around us. This experience was a dream come true! We swam around the corals and were relishing the experience when we suddenly heard a loud whistle. We looked around and found a big creature. It was a dolphin, whose tail was stuck between the corals. I and Zoya decided to help the dolphin. We moved the corals and they broke off releasing the dolphin's tail. The dolphin squealed with joy and came closer to us giving us a big hug.

When we turned to return back, the dolphin pushed us with its tail and started taking us along. We followed and it took us through different places and showed us the turtles, the octopuses and different sea creatures which were so beautiful. We were experiencing an amazing tour of the Andaman Sea. We soon stopped at a place filled with different types of shells. We took a few of them as a gift and the dolphin helped us locate the most beautiful ones. We were admiring this huge collection of shells and suddenly found the dolphin missing. We looked around but it was nowhere to be seen. We could hear its call somewhere nearby and went in that direction only to find it trapped in a net.

The net was moving upwards. We dived up and saw a motorboat. There were two fishermen having a conversation. We heard them secretly and got to know that they were illegally trying to ship this dolphin to an aquarium in Japan. We wanted to save our dear dolphin from these people. We swiftly worked out a plan! When the fishermen were busy in their conversation, I cried out for help pretending that I was drowning. The fishermen saw me and jumped to rescue me.

Meanwhile, Zoya got an opportunity to cut the net and rescue the dolphin. The fishermen returned and were shocked to see that their precious catch was missing. We returned to our boat and started sailing towards the shore. On our way back, we heard victory squeals and soon saw a pod of dolphins circle around our boat with joy. We danced with delight and captured this wonderful moment. The pod dispersed in some time, but we were in for a shock when we heard loud cries for help.

We quickly sailed towards the two men who were shouting for help. We rescued the two men who were none other than the fishermen who had caught the dolphin. We got to know from them that they were caught unawares when a large group of dolphins attacked their boat and overturned it. They were held in midst of a huge wave and were struggling to stay afloat when we sighted them. They thanked us for saving their lives.

We understood that the dolphins had worked out a plan to save themselves. The fishermen vowed to never set their sight on the dolphins again. Indeed, Life is the best teacher; it teaches us many valuable lessons!

XIII
KASHMIR – THE PARADISE

The Crown of our Country,
It's a Splendour of the North,
With its endless beauty,
It's a Paradise on Earth!
Land of the snowy mountains,
and the beautiful lakes,
Land of the green meadows,
and the freshness of flowers,
Here's the Paradise!
Land of the Aromatic Saffron,
and the melodious Santoor,
Land of the magnificent Chinars,
and the splendid Shikharas,
Here's Nature's bliss!
Land of the warm Pashminas,
and the woollen Namdas,
Land of Apple orchards,
and the chirping birds,
Here's the Paradise!

The warmth of its people,
and the beauty of its land,
Mesmerizes every visitor,
who hopes to return again,
It's a Paradise!

XIV
CORRUPTION CORRUPTS MEAL

Siva Karthikeyan, the collector of Krishna Nagar is well-known in the district. He is an honest and hardworking officer who would ensure that all the schemes and policies of the state government are properly executed in his district. He would resolve every issue diligently.

He is a bureaucrat who is always surrounded by his secretary and officials during his visits. People never get to openly share their grievances with him. They had to make do with whatever the officials directed them to speak to the collector.

One evening, Karthikeyan's wife, Padmavati was returning back from a wedding at Hosur. When her car stops at an IndianOil petrol pump, she notices young children with baskets running towards the vehicles. A young girl with curly hair, tattered clothes, and a basket of peanuts knocks at her car and requests Padmavati to buy some peanuts.

Padmavati looks at the girl and asks her if she goes to school. The girl tells her that she used to go to the Government school but would often fall sick because of the food and the filth there. Her poor parents got dejected and removed her from school. She now sells peanuts and helps her parents in the field to earn a living. Padmavati is shocked and enquires further to know what led to her discontinuation from school. The girl claims that the mid-day meal at her school is so awful that they would rather stay hungry than eat it! A large portion of the school is also used as a cattle shed.

Padmavati is taken aback. She assures the little girl that she will help her go back to school very soon. All along her way back, she keeps thinking of the little girl and the other poor children like her who are not benefitted by the government schemes. During dinner, a disturbed Padmavati narrates the little girl's plight to her husband. The collector is shocked to know the matter and informs his officials to plan a visit to the school.

The next day, when he visits the school for an inspection, he sees many children happily studying with clean surroundings and good meals being served to the children. He is happy to see the condition of the *school and tells Padmavati that the girl's story may not be true. Padmavati however isn't convinced.*

After a few days, Karthikeyan's son tells him that he learned about King Vikramaditya in his class and was impressed with the way in which the king reached out to his subjects in disguise. On hearing this, Karthikeyan is reminded of the poor girl's story and gets an idea of visiting the school in disguise to find out the truth. He goes to the school as a parent on the pretext of getting his son admitted. He is shocked to find more cows than students. The foul smell and the flies pester him a lot! He finds the classrooms empty and gets to know that the students were having their mid-day meal. As the authorities were busy with the admission process, he observes the condition of the meal being served to the students. He witnesses a few children being whipped when they complain about the food.

Karthikeyan gets to know the truth that the corrupt officials were feeding children stale food to save the funds given by the Government for their own comfort. He silently records the entire incident and shares it with the higher authorities. The corrupt officials and the headmaster are suspended. The story spreads and the people become vigilant about corruption. The collector opens a helpline for the public to directly reach out to him and help eradicate corruption.

The poor children happily get back to school and resume their studies. The collector announces that having schemes and policies for the betterment of the people isn't enough. The benefits have to reach the common man and for that, it is important that every citizen is vigilant and strengthens the society by uprooting corruption.

XV

SHIELD

It protects us from danger;
It helps us in a tough fight;
It guards us in every attack;
It saves us with all might;
It keeps us away from the enemy's sight!
It is our saviour;
It fights for us on the battlefield!
It keeps us safe;
It ensures that we are secure,
It guards us against our fear!
A Shield is our lifetime protector!!

XVI
THE SHRINK RAY

Though the street was silent, clinging sounds from Professor Naman's lab disturbed the neighbourhood's calm atmosphere. It was noon, but the Professor was so busy that his daughter Nanya had to serve the Professor lunch in his lab. She pushed the rusted gate of the lab and knocked the wooden door. When she didn't receive any reply, she entered angrily into the lab and was setting the dishes on the nearest table. She claimed, "Even on a Sunday, you have no intention to take some rest, father. It is almost thirty minutes past noon and you couldn't even come to the dining hall for lunch!" The Professor's new machine couldn't shrink the apple that was kept for testing his new shrink ray. He was in no mood to listen to Nanya as he was concentrating on solving the errors in the machine.

Suddenly, the machine shook and pointed out light rays directly over Nanya. On spotting Nanya just below the sparkling rays, the Professor shouted, "Nanya, move immediately from that place!" But it was too late, Nanya just disappeared! The machine worked in this trial and shrunk Nanya. A blow of wind gusted into the lab and Nanya just flew along with the blowing wind. She screamed as loud as she could but her sound was just like faint squeals. The Professor could hear them but couldn't spot tiny Nanya.

Nanya was flying far from her home. She was helpless in this state and continued to move until the wind stopped near some mushrooms in the forest. Nanya was happy as she could finally stand on some ground after a long journey flying in the blue, sunny sky. She observed the mushrooms surrounding her and found windows and doors cut on them. She felt as if this was a dream but then a small rock hit her and she realised that all of this was real.

Tiny kids were playing cricket with the rock nearby. The tiny kids first stared at Nanya, and then apologised. A group of tiny people soon joined the kids and introduced themselves to the unknown visitor Nanya, who was witnessing a settlement of the smallest people on earth for the very first time in her young life. The people called themselves Dwarflets. An old Dwarflet who appeared as the leader of the Dwarflets invited Nanya for tea in his mushroom.

Just as Nanya sat on the cosy sofa in the mushroom, the small village started shaking vigorously. Nanya wondered if it was an earthquake, but then saw a giant boy approaching the Dwarflets. The leader told Nanya to hide in his mushroom and then ordered the

Dwarflets to handle the giant boy. The Dwarflets served the boy with loads of delicious-looking delicacies. After completing the large meal, the boy picked each Dwarflet and started shooting them with his slingshot. On hearing the Dwarflets scream in fear, the boy started laughing loudly, he was enjoying but the Dwarflets were hurt.

After the troublesome boy left, the leader who was called Old Donald, explained to Nanya that the boy would come daily and treat the Dwarflets with disrespect for his amusement. Nanya pitied the Dwarflets and came up with a plan to teach the boy a lesson for ever. They tied a thick rope to the entrance of the tiny village. When the boy came the next day, he fell after tripping over the tied rope. Then, they tied his whole-body flat to the ground and fed him huge amounts of food. The boy couldn't eat any further. He applied all his strength and broke the ropes tied over him. The Dwarflets got scared, but the boy changed his behaviour and apologized to them for all the trouble he had caused and also promised that he would never return again.

The Dwarflets thanked Nanya, but another gust of wind took Nanya away towards the town market before she could bid "Goodbye!" to the Dwarflets. Nanya landed on the pathway in the market. She feared that she would be stamped by the people walking around in the market but the owner of a toy shop found Nanya and mistook her for a mini figurine. He kept her for display in his store. Nanya was waiting for the right moment and started walking away from *the display area when no customers were noticing her. On reaching the shop entrance, a man with a little boy accompanying him, spotted her and carried her away. Nanya saw that it was her father, Professor Naman with her cousin, Rakesh who was visiting them from the USA after many years.*

Professor Naman took Nanya back to the lab. He reversed the switch of his shrink ray and brought Nanya back to her original height. She narrated all the happenings she had witnessed when she was tiny as an ant. While nobody at home believed Nanya's story, little Rakesh was eager to meet the Dwarflets. He was behind Nanya persuading her to show him those tiny people. Meanwhile, Old Donald unveiled a statue of Nanya in the Dwarflets' village to always remember the one who had saved them from the cruel boy.

XVII
TAMIL NADU - THE TRADITION!

Mornings filled with freshness,
The aroma of the Coffee beans,
Doorsteps adorned with Kolams,
The music of Suprabhatams!
The fragrance of the Mallipoos,
The colourful Kanjivarams,
Greetings of Namaskarams,
The ringing of the temple bells!
The aroma of the Sambar,
Music of the Nadhaswarams,
The tune of Bharatnatyam,
Spirit of Carnatic in the air!
Sumptuous spread on the banana leaves,
Gopurams of the temples,
A legacy passed on generations,
Manifested in the vibrant traditions,
This is our Tamil Nadu, my friends!!

XVIII
HUNTER ROBERT RETURNS

It was a bright sunny morning. Hunter Robert was feeding his leopard Greta. Just then, Mr. Johnson entered with a terrifying news. He informed the hunter that the Forest Officials had started allowing tourists into the forest. It was an order by the King of Jabalpur, Maharajah Gopal Singh II to earn revenue from the tourism industry. Paths were laid for the tourists to explore the forest. Mr. Johnson feared that the hunter's secret abode might be discovered. Hunter Robert realised that the animals were not safe anymore. He feared that the poachers could disguise as tourists and hunt the animals.

Hunter Robert decided to go to the city of Jabalpur and make the King understand that the safety of animals was more important than earning revenue. Mr. Johnson was not happy with the hunter's decision as the Maharajah never heeded to the advice of others and was cruel to people who spoke against him. But Hunter Robert had already made up his mind.

He rode on a horse all the way to the magnificent palace of Jabalpur, the Vasant Vilas. The people just couldn't believe that the brave hunter had finally returned after many years! The Maharajah was also surprised to meet Robert after a long time and gave him a huge welcome. After the celebrations, the Maharajah enquired, "You never return without the animal you set off to hunt." The hunter said, "I am sorry, Your Highness. Mother Nature could no longer see the animals getting killed and taught me the importance of nature while I was hunting the leopard. I am no longer a hunter now. I am a protector of Mother Nature and I safeguard the animals."

The Maharajah was shocked and said, "Robert, you know that nature is dangerous. You yourself saw the leopard killing our people." Robert exclaimed, "Your Highness, the people she killed were all poachers. You encouraged hunting of poor animals and took it as a sport. The animals had no choice but to harm people and defend themselves." On hearing Robert speak against the monarch, the Maharajah's greedy advisor, Shanti Prasad, whispered to the Maharajah to order the arrest of the hunter.

Robert knew that Shanti Prasad must have tricked the Maharajah to arrest people who were against the orders of the monarch. He had to escape and he sped *away immediately on his horse before the guards could arrest him. Shanti Prasad then informed the Maharajah that Robert would surely reach the place where he protected all the animals. They could chase him and hunt all the animals. The soldiers were ordered to chase Robert with their weapons. Robert was safe until a sharp arrow struck his arm.*

He managed to reach home before the soldiers but fainted at the doorstep. On seeing her master in pain, his pet leopard, Greta thinks of a plan to save him. The soldiers get lost in the bushes and the Maharajah ordered them to cut all the trees until Robert is caught. Greta rushed to the majestic Lion King, Sher Shah, and requested him to help her master. Sher Shah ordered all the animals to assemble near the waterfall. Soon, the army of soldiers and hunters led by Shanti Prasad and the Maharajah reached there.

Robert then told the story of each of his beloved animals, "Rajah Saheb, you see this lion king, his lioness was killed. These pair of elephants lost their young son to a hunter. These cubs lost their parents while it was you who hunted them. Now, try replacing their lost ones with your own family. Wouldn't you feel sorrow if you lost your own family and saw them getting killed?"

The Maharajah was silent for a while and then his eyes were filled with tears. Meanwhile, Shanti Prasad who was aiming his arrow at Sher Shah was stopped by the Maharajah and everyone was ordered to drop their bows and arrows. The Maharajah finally understood that he was hurting the magical beauty of Mother Nature. He realised that it was Shanti Prasad who had turned him into an evil person. He banished his own advisor and took back his order of allowing tourists to venture the forests. He joined Hunter Robert's campaign to protect the animals' privacy.

The Maharajah requested Robert to come and live with him in the royal palace as his trusted advisor. But Robert refused. He told the Maharajah that he enjoyed living in the forest in midst of the greenery and wildlife but promised that he would always be there to give him advice when he needed it the most.

XIX
NEWSPAPER

The morning sun glistens
The whole world awakes
And the newspaper arrives!
With a newspaper in hand,
How refreshing the morning tea tastes!
With every turn of a page,
It introduces us to the developing times
Informs us about crimes,
Gives a peek into the world's ups and downs,
Features the world's joys and sorrows
Takes us into the amazing world of entertainment and sports,
Gives us a glimpse of the world's tidings.
Reading the newspaper,
It's an addiction of every reader,
Adds value to one's persona,
Our bond is inseparable,
Its immense perks are immeasurable!
Its our best friend, Our relationship will never end,
As a new daily get published,
Our knowledge about current affairs gets replenished!

XX
HUNTER ROBERT STARTS PHOTOGRAPHY!

It was a bright and sunny day. Hunter Robert Williams was surveying the forest with his leopard Greta. Just then, Mr. Johnson, his friend and hardworking assistant came along with a man. On seeing Hunter Robert, the man was very excited and hugged him. Robert was at first surprised but then he recognized Roshan, his old friend. Roshan was the one who had earlier helped Robert get hunting assignments and make a living.

Robert and Roshan walked through the green bushes reminiscing the earlier days and returned to Robert's humble abode in the forest. While relishing a cup of tea under the shade of a huge banyan tree, Roshan enquired, "How do you make a living, dear Robert?

Campaigning for the protection of animals will not help you earn." Robert said that he used the nature's resources to fulfil his needs and hence, he did not require money for living a comfortable life. But he further added that he at times needed money for campaigning in other areas and spreading awareness about the safety of animals.

Roshan suggested that Robert should take up some work. As Robert was not willing to leave the forest, Roshan suggested that he could try his hand at Wildlife Photography and participate in Photography competitions. In this way, Robert could use the prize money in protecting nature and wildlife.

Robert started off by first trying to take a picture of a crocodile but the crocodile lifted its tail and splashed water on Robert. Robert returned home wet and was hesitant to try again. Roshan encouraged Robert to try capturing the flying birds in his photo. Robert found a pair of parrots the next morning and chased them for a picture but with no success. All of a sudden, a herd of elephants came running in the same path and all the mud and dirt of the path splashed on Robert as the elephants passed by. Robert came home late that evening all covered in dirt and with no luck. He decided to give up wildlife photography. Roshan then planned to take help of Murali, a wildlife photographer. Murali agreed happily as it would be the first time he was teaching photography to someone. He looked forward to working with the great Robert Williams.

The next day, Murali visited Robert and started taking lessons in the art of photography. He shared various tricks to perfectly capture animals in a photo. He advised Robert to stay hidden while taking the photograph as the flash and sound of the camera disturbed the animals. He also told him to maintain silence of the surroundings during the photoshoot so that the animals did not sense him. Finally, he also told him to capture the photograph of birds by first attracting them towards some fruits and water. Soon under Murali's excellent training, Robert mastered the art of Wildlife Photography.

Murali was extremely happy! Robert thanked him for his training and said that he would now try his best and not let him down. Robert became an ace in photography with his hard work and constant effort. He participated in his first wildlife photography competition and surprisingly, his photograph got selected by the judges. Murali congratulated Robert on his spectacular achievement.

Robert continued participating in various photography competitions and won many accolades with his talent. This way he continued to live in the forest as well as get funds from the prize money for campaigning for the protection of animals. He became a well-known photographer and his photographs started appearing in magazines and newspapers across the world.

Robert now wished that his photographs could bring some change in the world. He then remembered that every time he visited the city, he would notice a lot of pollution. He felt he could highlight the ill effects of pollution through his photographs to help create awareness among the people. To achieve this, he took the help of Ramamurthy, who worked for a leading magazine company. His photos of polluted environment got published alongside the photos of a clean, beautiful and pollution-free environment in the leading magazines. Everyone started talking about his photographs and soon the public realized the harm pollution was causing to their environment and how beautiful it was to live in a clean and pollution-free environment.

The copies of the magazine soon reached the global market and all the leaders world over came together to join Robert's campaign against pollution. Several young youths volunteered to clean the lakes and their surroundings. Robert was filled with joy as the people had started discovering ways to stop pollution. They stopped the piling of garbage in rivers and lakes. Farmers reduced the usage of chemical fertilizers and pesticides. Solar panels were fitted on many rooftops and people started the use of solar energy on a large scale. Electric and battery-operated transport replaced the vehicles which emitted smoke and caused pollution.

Robert had successfully accomplished his target through his insightful photographs. He became a popular figure and was also interviewed by various news channels. In one such interview to a journalist of the National News Network, Robert reiterated the famous saying of Mother Teresa – 'One cannot change the world alone, but one can cast a stone across the waters to create many ripples.'

• 57 •

XXI

THE SCOOTER THIEF

It was a wonderful evening and the weather was very pleasant. My family was engaged in the daily chores and I was completing my maths assignment. My dad was held up in a meeting and had not yet returned home. My mom and grandma were busy cooking delicious dinner for the day.

Suddenly, my grandma heard a loud noise and saw that someone was taking away a scooter, which looked like the one my mom possessed. She called out loudly so the thief would get scared, but he scurried away on the scooter. Mom quickly surveyed the CCTV footage and could capture a blurry image of the thief.

The scooter was very dear our family as it was gifted by my great-grandmother. We set off on a search for the scooter along with our neighbour, Mr. Mohan who volunteered to help us.

We enquired from the nearby traffic police who immediately recollected having seen the scooter. He had chased the rider for driving in the wrong direction but couldn't get hold of him and only managed to note its number plate.

Mom and my grandma started looking out for him in the direction pointed by the constable. On the way, Mr. Mohan noticed a person with a scooter just like the one stolen. He grabbed the person and started questioning, only to be disappointed to find that it had a different number plate.

The long search continued in the late evening. Manoeuvring through the various lanes and after enquiring from many small shops, we got a lead. A shop owner could match the CCTV image with a young chap working in a nearby eatery. We took him along and continued our search. We reached the eatery with great hope, but got to know that this worker had left early. We were returning back discussing how to proceed, when suddenly we spotted the scooter in a garage. The garage owner informed us that the scooter was brought by two youth who had negotiated the price to sell it and were to return at closing time to get the money.

It was shop closing time and we eagerly waited for the thieves to return. They came happily to get their money and were caught by Mr. Mohan. While everyone was engrossed in questioning one of them, his accomplice tried to run off but was caught by the alert garage owner. Mr. Mohan handed over the thieves to the police.

The thieves explained that they were from a poor family and did petty jobs for money. They couldn't earn enough to provide for their family and resorted to stealing. Our Grandma felt pity for them, she thought that punishment will make them understand their mistake, so they were jailed for a week.

Grandma, my mom and Mr. Mohan returned back home with the Chetak. Grandpa heard the thieves' story and felt sorry for the poor. The next day, he narrated the incident to his MLA friend and suggested that vocational training and job opportunities be provided to the poor youth. The humble MLA took this matter to the Chief Minister who agreed to start the project and donated funds for it.

XXII
RAINBOW

The vibrant colors of a rainbow,
They represent pride,
They bring up a smile,
They spread a message of peace,
They initiate a positive vibe,
They suggest - "All colors equally shine,
but each of them are unique"
They influence and inspire all,
to work together and unite,
and change the world,
making the future bright!

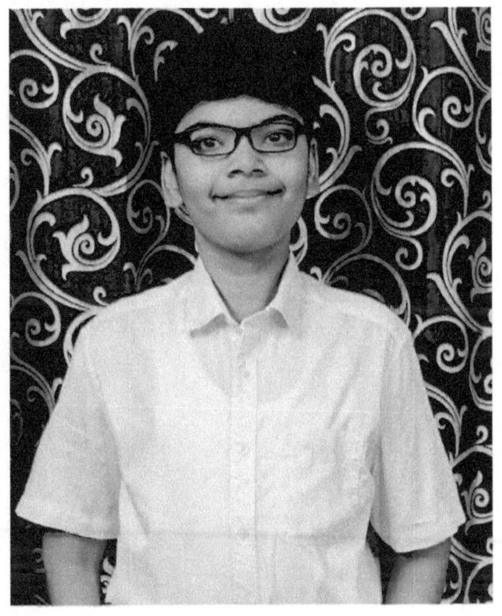

M Farhaan Hussain

Farhaan is a young author with a passion for writing short stories and poems. He is a student of Asan Memorial Senior Secondary School. He loves reading books and writes fiction stories for young readers. He is also keenly interested in Robotics and Artificial Intelligence. He loves to work on his project ideas and showcase them on his YouTube channel.